THE LITTLE FIR TREE

Re-told by Anne McKie. Illustrated by Ken McKie.

Once upon a time, in a clearing deep in the middle of a great forest, there grew a Little Fir Tree.

All around him were giant pine trees with long straight trunks, their top branches almost reaching the sky - well at least, that's how it looked to the Little Fir Tree, who longed to grow tall and tower over the whole forest.

The animals who lived nearby loved the Little Fir Tree. In spring and summer they played all day beneath his soft feathery branches. Small birds built their nests amongst his sweet smelling needles, sheltered from the strong winds that swept through the giant pines high above.

All day long, the Little Fir Tree could hear the sound of axes ringing through the forest, as the woodcutters felled the tallest trees and brought them crashing to the ground.

The Little Fir Tree sighed to himself: "I wish my trunk was tall and straight enough to be a ship's mast, or even the strongest beam in a big house!"

With that, he stretched his small branches as hard as he could, to try and make himself grow a bit bigger.

One day, the wind that swayed the Little Fir Tree's branches began to grow colder and the first few snowflakes of winter started to fall.

The animals all disappeared for their long winter sleep, and most of the birds had flown away to summer lands. Very soon the snow lay thick on the ground - even the woodcutters had left the forest until next spring.

Was the Little Fir Tree lonely? Oh, no! For soon new exciting sounds began to fill the air. It was the laughter and shrieks of happy children, as they tobogganed down the forest's snowy slopes.

All of a sudden the Little Fir Tree was surrounded by
three delighted children. They danced around him in the
snow, clapping and singing. "We've found the most
beautiful tree in the forest," they chorused.

The Little Fir Tree, his branches sparkling and twinkling
with frost, almost blushed with pride.

"Father! Come quickly!" all three cried together. "Here
is our Christmas Tree!"

Before he knew what was happening, the Little Fir Tree
had been cut down and gently placed on a sled. Very
soon he was speeding along between the great trunks of
the giant pines, until the forest was left far behind.

Everyone seemed so delighted with the Little Fir Tree
that he felt happy too.

At last they came to the small town at the foot of the forest's slopes.

As the children ran through the streets, they shouted to everybody they met, "Look at our tree! Isn't it the most perfect Christmas Tree you ever saw?"

The Little Fir Tree felt rather puzzled. "What on earth is a Christmas Tree?" he thought to himself.

The Little Fir Tree was beginning to enjoy himself. "This is much better than becoming one of those giant pine trees and living all your life in the forest."

"Where did you get that lovely little tree?" "Is he for sale?" "Please can I buy him?" people shouted as they passed by. The three children just grinned and shook their heads.

All at once, the Little Fir Tree looked around. He saw fir trees everywhere! They were standing in windows, outside front doors, on porches and in gardens.

"These must be Christmas Trees!" smiled the Little Fir Tree, feeling proud. "Then I shall be the very best Christmas Tree of all!"

When the Little Fir Tree reached the children's house,
he was carefully carried inside and placed upright in a tub.
That night, the whole family gathered round to decorate
their Christmas Tree - for it was Christmas Eve.

Everyone helped to hang the decorations on the Little Fir Tree's branches. Soon this very special little tree was covered with toys and fruit, cookies and candy, and lots of tiny candles. And at the very top - a golden star!

There stood the Little Fir Tree quivering with pride. He really was the Most Beautiful Christmas Tree in the World!

The tiny candles twinkled like a thousand stars and filled the room with their sparkling light. The Little Fir Tree shone in all his glory, for it was Christmas Eve - the most magical night of the year.

Before they went to bed on this very special night, the children left their stockings beneath the Little Fir Tree. "No one has ever seen Santa Claus," whispered the children, very excited, "and he won't come until everyone is fast asleep."

But late that night Santa Claus did come. He slipped silently into the room, quietly took the children's presents from his sack and popped them underneath the tree.

Just for a moment he stepped back to admire the beautiful Little Fir Tree. He gave a broad smile, a twinkle of his eye, then vanished up the chimney.

The Little Fir Tree felt so happy to be a Christmas Tree, and very proud that he alone had really seen Santa Claus.

During the twelve days of Christmas, the Little Fir Tree had a wonderful time. Many visitors called at the house to admire him, and lots of children came in from the street to see how beautiful he looked. The Little Fir Tree loved every moment of it, and thought it would last forever.

All too soon Twelfth Night came, which marked the end of Christmas.

Every single decoration in the house was taken down and packed away until next year.

The Little Fir Tree looked so bare. Lots of his needles had dropped onto the floor and his branches were brittle and dry. Worse was to come! Along with all the other old greenery in the house, the poor Little Fir Tree was taken outside and burned on the bonfire.

And that was the end of the Little Fir Tree!

The whole family felt sorry that Christmas was over and that their lovely tree had met such a sad end. So there and then, the children's father made a promise that it would not happen again.

During the long cold months of winter that followed,
the family never forgot their Little Fir Tree. The children
remembered his dazzling brilliance, and it made them feel
happy through the dark winter nights.

Spring came at last! The warm sun melted the snow and
ice and the forest came to life once more.

One bright sunny morning, Father took the three
children to the spot where he had cut down the Little Fir
Tree.

This time he took with him a spade and not an axe.
Together they carefully dug up three trees - one for each of
the children; a tiny tree, a middle size tree and one a bit **bigger**.

Back home they planted the biggest tree in the garden, the middle size one near the house, and the tiny tree in a pot near the door.

So when next Christmas came they would have fir trees that would keep growing, and not have to be thrown out and burned like the poor Little Fir Tree!

As the years went by, the children decorated their trees every Christmas. On the two outside, they tied hundreds of glistening lamps. The smallest tree was carried inside every year until it grew too big for the house.

Now the children have grown up and have children of their own - and grandchildren. The three fir trees have grown, and now they are the tallest in the valley. And every Christmas Eve, they shine so brightly, for all the world to see.